A Note to Parents and Caregivers:

Read-it! Readers are for children who are just starting on the amazing road to reading. These beautiful books support both the acquisition of reading skills and the love of books.

 The PURPLE LEVEL presents basic topics and objects using high frequency words and simple language patterns.

 The RED LEVEL presents familiar topics using common words and repeating sentence patterns.

 The BLUE LEVEL presents new ideas using a larger vocabulary and varied sentence structure.

 The YELLOW LEVEL presents more challenging ideas, a broad vocabulary, and wide variety in sentence structure.

 The GREEN LEVEL presents more complex ideas, an extended vocabulary range, and expanded language structures.

 The ORANGE LEVEL presents a wide range of ideas and concepts using challenging vocabulary and complex language structures.

When sharing a book with your child, read in short stretches, pausing often to talk about the pictures. Have your child turn the pages and point to the pictures and familiar words. And be sure to reread favorite stories or parts of stories.

There is no right or wrong way to share books with children. Find time to read with your child, and pass on the legacy of literacy.

Adria F. Klein, Ph.D.
Professor Emeritus
California State University
San Bernardino, California

Editor: Christianne Jones
Page Production: Tracy Kaehler
Creative Director: Keith Griffin
Editorial Director: Carol Jones

First American edition published in 2006 by
Picture Window Books
5115 Excelsior Boulevard
Suite 232
Minneapolis, MN 55416
877-845-8392
www.picturewindowbooks.com

First published in 2005 by
Allegra Publishing Limited
Unit 13/15 Quayside Lodge
William Morris Way
Townmead Road
London SW6 2UZ UK

Printed in the United States of America.

Library of Congress Cataloging-in-Publication Data
Law, Felicia.
Rumble meets Randy Rabbit / by Felicia Law ; illustrated by Yoon-Mi Pak.
p. cm. — (Read-it! readers)
Summary: Rumble hires Randy Rabbit to turn part of the jungle surrounding his
Cave Hotel into a garden so that he can pick flowers for Penny Panther, but soon
Rumble and Shelby Spider are wondering if Randy Rabbit planted anything other
than carrots.
ISBN 1-4048-1337-3 (hard cover)
[1. Gardening—Fiction. 2. Rabbits—Fiction. 3. Dragons—Fiction. 4. Spiders—
Fiction.] I. Pak, Yoon Mi, ill. II. Title. III. Series.

PZ7.L41835Rumr 2005
[E]—dc22   2005027182

Rumble Meets Randy Rabbit

by Felicia Law
illustrated by Yoon-Mi Pak

Special thanks to our advisers for their expertise:

Adria F. Klein, Ph.D.
Professor Emeritus, California State University
San Bernardino, California

Susan Kesselring, M.A.
Literacy Educator
Rosemount–Apple Valley–Eagan (Minnesota) School District

PICTURE WINDOW BOOKS
Minneapolis, Minnesota

This is the life of a cool, young dragon named Rumble. When his grandma leaves her run-down cave to him, Rumble sets about making it into a four-star hotel. He doesn't do it all alone. He has help from a picky hotel inspector and an annoying spider named Shelby.

Rumble wants to plant beautiful flowers for Penny Panther, but he doesn't know how. That's when Randy Rabbit, the gardener, arrives. Randy appears to know what he's doing, but will any flowers grow in Rumble's new garden?

Rumble had a problem. He wanted to pick a large bunch of flowers for Penny Panther. She had such pretty green eyes.

But the garden at Rumble's Cave Hotel didn't have any flowers. It had no flowers, no berries, and no fruits. It was a mess!

So it was Rumble's lucky day when Randy Rabbit arrived.

"Dig, dig, dig," said Randy. "Are you looking for a gardener?"

"I am," Rumble said. "Can you start right away? I really need some flowers."

"Dig, dig, dig," said Randy.

"What's he talking about?" asked Shelby Spider.

"I don't know," said Rumble. "I just hope he's a good gardener."

"Here's the garden," said Rumble.

"Where's the garden?" asked Randy.

"It's right here," said Rumble, "under the thistles, thorns, leaves, and weeds."

"Hoe, hoe, hoe," said Randy.

"Ho, ho, ho?" repeated Shelby. "What's he laughing about?"

"I don't know," said Rumble. "I just hope he's a good gardener."

"Leave everything to me," said Randy. "I'll get this garden started. I'll plant rows and rows of carrots."

"I don't like carrots," said Rumble.

"A garden's not a garden without carrots," said Randy Rabbit.

"I want flowers," said Rumble, "with big, bright petals."

"I want flowers, too," said Shelby. "Flowers attract insects, and I like insects."

"Carrots and pumpkins, carrots and peas, carrots and tomatoes—I will grow these," sang Randy.

"You'll have to put your foot down if you want flowers," Shelby told Rumble.

Randy Rabbit hoed and dug up the weeds. He planted lots of seeds in neat rows.

"That rabbit knows what he's doing," Rumble said to Shelby. "The garden looks like a garden."

"The garden looks like rows of carrots," said Shelby. "Perhaps you should check."

"When will the flowers start to grow?" Rumble asked Randy.

"When the rain stops," said Randy.

"How long before the insects come?" asked Shelby. "There are still no insects."

"Good!" said Randy. "Most insects are pests."

"Most insects are delicious," said Shelby.

14

After the rain, the seeds started to grow.
Tiny, green shoots appeared above the soil.
Thick, green leaves started to sprout.

"Are these flowers?" asked Rumble.

"Of course," said Randy.

"That's odd. They look like carrots to me,"
said Shelby.

"All flowers look like carrots at first,"
said Randy.

"I really need flowers for Penny Panther," said Rumble.

"You must be patient," said Randy. "It takes time for flowers to grow."

"I can wait," said Rumble. "In fact, I'll sit down and wait right here."

"Plants won't grow any quicker just because you sit and watch them," said Randy.

But Rumble, Shelby, and Randy sat and watched the garden anyway.

"I told you they wouldn't grow any faster," said Randy.

"The flowers may grow tonight,"
said Rumble.

"I don't think so," said Randy. "But if
it makes you happy, I'll watch the flowers
all night, too."

"That's funny," said Rumble the next morning. "The flowers are growing smaller, not bigger. At this rate, I'll never have any flowers to give to Penny Panther."

"They still look like carrots to me," said Shelby Spider.

"Carrots, flowers, flowers, carrots," said Randy. "It's all the same in the end."

"I don't trust this rabbit," said Shelby. "He doesn't know his carrots from his flowers."

23

Rumble was still worried. "Perhaps someone is stealing the flowers," he said, shaking his head.

"Well, I'm not sitting here guarding flowers all day," said Shelby. "We'll stick a scarecrow in the ground. It will guard the flowers for us."

"Guard them from what?" asked Rumble.

"Birds," said Shelby.

"But birds don't steal flowers," said Rumble.

"They steal the insects on the flowers," said Shelby, "and the insects are all mine."

The scarecrow was made from two poles, a turnip, old clothes, and straw.

It stood in the garden looking very fierce, and it certainly scared away the crows.

"The scarecrow will protect the flowers and the insects," said Rumble.

"You're right," said Randy Rabbit. "Nobody will come near your flowers now. They'll be much too scared."

But the scarecrow didn't protect the flowers. When Rumble and Shelby arrived at the garden the next day, the neat rows of flowers were destroyed. The tops were all nibbled, and many of the rows had completely disappeared.

Randy Rabbit shrugged his shoulders. "I don't know," he said. "Maybe one scarecrow wasn't scary enough. I know a lot of animals who'd steal carrots. But flowers? Who'd want to steal flowers?"

"Take my advice," said Randy Rabbit. "Give Penny Panther some carrots. Everyone likes carrots. I've grown some very big carrots with yellow tops over there."

"Good idea," said Rumble.

"And the insects are very big, too. Come and see," said Randy.

"You're right," said Shelby. "I guess you are a good gardener after all."

More *Read-it!* Readers

Bright pictures and fun stories help you practice your reading skills. Look for more books at your level.

Alex and Sarah 1-4048-1352-7
Alex and the Team Jersey 1-4048-1024-2
Alex and Toolie 1-4048-1027-7
Clever Cat 1-4048-0560-5
Felicio's Incredible Invention 1-4048-1030-7
Flora McQuack 1-4048-0561-3
Izzie's Idea 1-4048-0644-X
Joe's Day at Rumble's Cave Hotel 1-4048-1339-X
Naughty Nancy 1-4048-0558-3
Parents Do the Weirdest Things! 1-4048-1031-5
The Princess and the Frog 1-4048-0562-1
The Princess and the Tower 1-4048-1184-2
Rumble Meets Harry Hippo 1-4048-1338-1
Rumble Meets Lucas Lizard 1-4048-1334-9
Rumble Meets Shelby Spider 1-4048-1286-5
Rumble Meets Todd Toad 1-4048-1340-3
Rumble Meets Vikki Viper 1-4048-1342-X
Rumble the Dragon's Cave 1-4048-1353-5
Rumble's Famous Granny 1-4048-1336-5
The Truth About Hansel and Gretel 1-4048-0559-1
Willie the Whale 1-4048-0557-5

Looking for a specific title or level? A complete list of *Read-it!* Readers is available on our Web site:
www.picturewindowbooks.com